Amanda Greenleaf and the Spell of the Water Witch

The author acknowledges the support of the Newfoundland and Labrador Arts Council.

Moonstone Press gratefully acknowledges support from the Ontario Arts Council in the publication of this book.

Art Production: Brian Brygier, St. Catharines, Ontario
Typesetting: Kim Yungblut, St. Catharines, Ontario
Printing: Hignell Printing Ltd., Winnipeg, Manitoba

Canadian Cataloguing in Publication Data

Kavanagh, Ed, 1954-
Amanda Greenleaf and the spell of the water witch

ISBN 0-920259-12-X

I. Udell, Janice. II. Title.

PS8571.A86A73 1987 jC813'.54 C87-093626-3
PZ7.K38Am 1987

Moonstone Press
46 Nelson Street West
Goderich, Ontario
Canada N7A 2M3

Amanda Greenleaf and the Spell of the Water Witch

ED KAVANAGH

Illustrated by Janice Udell

For Peter and Brenda,
Ursula and Anne

Chapter 1

Beneath the deep swirling water near a beautiful silver waterfall, Greta and Glinka were swimming together in a lovely underwater ballet. Their bodies curled and twisted in the most intricate ways, yet they mirrored each other's movements perfectly. Occasionally, they broke the surface and slapped the water with their turquoise tails. As they spun and somersaulted, Greta's long hair blossomed like an underwater cloud, and Glinka's tail seemed a young willow bending in a watery wind. But although their movements were light and pretty, their faces were serious and thoughtful. Presently, they dove to the deepest part of the pool and hovered, facing each other.

"The time has come," Glinka the merman said.

The little mermaid nodded her head sadly. "Yes, I know. How much time do we have?"

"Not long; only until the moon is full again. Already the water feels different — have you noticed?"

"Yes. It's *tingly* somehow."

"I think we should leave very soon," Glinka said firmly.

"Does Amanda Greenleaf know we must return?" Greta asked.

"I don't think so," Glinka replied. "I didn't tell her. I guess I didn't want to talk about it."

"Do you think she'll be unhappy?" asked Greta.

"I don't know. I'm a little unhappy — aren't you?"

"Oh yes," Greta sighed. "Amanda Greenleaf is the best friend we've ever had. I hope she understands."

Glinka smiled and took Greta's hand. Slowly they began to rise to the surface. "You're right," he said. "She is the best friend we've ever had. So she'll definitely understand. And, besides, it's just for a little while — it's not as if we were leaving forever."

"And it will be nice to go home for a visit," said Greta. "It's so different from here."

"It's certainly bigger," laughed Glinka. "Wouldn't it be nice if she could come with us?"

"It would be wonderful. But you know how she feels about this place. She is Guardian of the Waterfall; her place is here. And she's so busy these days with her music."

"Not to mention her musical instruments," added Glinka. "She's always inventing new ones."

Greta and Glinka reached the surface and leaped in perfect arcs through the cool air. The waterfall thundered down around them.

"We'd better go tell her now," suggested Greta. "I wonder where she is."

In her house behind the waterfall, Amanda Greenleaf was about to test her latest creation. In her hands she held a beautifully curled piece of wood which she had found in the forest and fitted with strings of different lengths. "Well," she said expectantly, "I hope this works," and she gently brushed her hand across the strings. Clear crystal notes jumped out, and they were so pure that Amanda Greenleaf couldn't believe anything could be so lovely.

"It works!" she cried happily. "I knew it would!" She tried the strings again, and soon she was playing a spritely little melody. "Oh, it's wonderful! It's different than my flute, but in its own way it's just as beautiful."

"Amanda Greenleaf!" two voices called from outside. "Can you come out, please? We have to talk to you."

"Oh, that's Greta and Glinka. I must show them my new ... my new what?" she wondered. She thought for a moment and then she knew. "I know. I'll call it a harp."

Amanda Greenleaf stood up and gathered the harp lovingly into her arms. Then she covered it up carefully so it wouldn't get wet, and stepped out through the falling curtain of water that was her front door. She looked very pretty. Her dress was a beautiful green and her golden hair shone in the sun.

A silver chain and green leaf graced her neck, the chain and leaf that gave her the powers due the Guardian of the Waterfall. With it she could swim and live in the water as easily as the merpeople, and because of it she knew there was a spirit in the water, and that the water was living and precious. Sometimes, she talked to the Water Spirit and learned that the rivers and streams were delicate, and that they must be taken care of.

"There you are," said Greta when Amanda Greenleaf appeared. "You're busier than a little bee these days. Don't you ever take time for some relaxation?"

Amanda Greenleaf laughed. "But I enjoy my work so much. It's such an adventure. There's nothing more thrilling than finishing a new instrument and testing it for the first time. Of course, it doesn't always work, but when it does ... when it does I feel all filled up with light — filled to bursting!"

"Amanda Greenleaf, we have something very important to tell you," Glinka said seriously.

But Amanda Greenleaf was so excited about her new harp that she hardly heard him. "Why, this new instrument is just exquisite," she said.

"But we have to ..."

"I'm going to call it a harp."

"Amanda Greenleaf, there's something ..."

"Would you like to hear it?" she asked eagerly.

"But Amanda ..."

"Oh, it's wonderful! The sounds are so pure."

"Amanda Greenleaf, we have to leave you!" Greta and Glinka cried together.

Amanda Greenleaf laid down the harp and looked closely at her friends. There was a puzzled expression on her face.

"You have to leave? But why? You're not upset with me, are you? I know I've been busy with my music. Have I neglected you?"

"No, it's not that," Greta said softly. "We understand about your music. It's ... oh, you explain, Glinka."

Glinka looked very thoughtful. "Amanda Greenleaf, even though we have lived in this beautiful river with you and been your friends, there is still a lot you don't know about us. Merpeople have a great fondness for secrets, and besides, we could never tell you everything there is to know — our customs and habits, dreams and needs. Merpeople are magical and ... well, there are certain things we must do."

"Yes," said Amanda Greenleaf. "I understand."

"You see," said Greta, "we didn't always live in this river. We had been here only a little while ourselves when you first came. We found this river and waterfall when we were exploring. It was because of you that we stayed."

"You taught us so much," said Glinka. "It was hard to leave and go back home."

"But I don't understand," said Amanda Greenleaf. "If this isn't your home, where is it?"

Glinka smiled. "This river is a living thing; it never stops flowing. But there is a time and place where it ceases to be the river — when it becomes something more, something much bigger. That's the way of all rivers."

Amanda Greenleaf nodded in agreement. "I know about that," she said. "The Water Spirit told me that the water flows on and on until it reaches ..."

"The ocean," said Greta. "The ocean is our home."

"And we must always return to it," Glinka said.

"I see," said Amanda Greenleaf. "You must be homesick for the ocean. Is that why you want to go back?"

"Well, partly," smiled Greta. "But we have no choice. We absolutely must go back — if only for a little while."

Glinka cupped some water in his hands and held it up to Amanda Greenleaf. "You see, the water in your river and waterfall is not like the water in the ocean. This water is fresh, but the ocean water is salt. Merpeople can only live in the river water for a certain length of time. Then they must return to the ocean. Really, we should have left days ago."

"I understand," said Amanda Greenleaf. "But what would happen if you didn't go back, if you stayed in the river?"

Greta and Glinka glanced at each other nervously. Neither of them wanted to say. Finally Greta gathered herself together. "Among the merpeople there is a poem that describes what happens if we don't return to the ocean."

Greta and Glinka moved closer together and recited:

The merfolk of the swelling sea
Who swim its depths and call it home
The merfolk with their turquoise tails
The merfolk with their golden combs
Are free to roam if so they please
But one thing they must not forget
If ever they leave their salty home
They must return to the swelling sea
Or else they'll turn to frothy foam
So when the moon begins to grow
Remember the sea — the sea's your home

"Now do you understand?" asked Greta. "We have to go back. If we don't, we'll lose our strength and form and become foam upon the water, drifting wherever it takes us, forever."

Amanda Greenleaf listened carefully, a serious expression on her face.

"Then, of course, you must leave," she said. "I'll miss you," she added gently.

"We'll miss you, too," said Glinka. "But we'll come back soon. We promise."

"And that's another special thing about merpeople," Greta laughed. "They never break their promises."

Chapter 2

Under the cold moonlight the river wound its way swiftly through the hilly, wooded land. Beneath the surface of the river many creatures lived and hardly knew that a moon shone above them. There were plants silently swaying in the undulating water, or clinging noiselessly among the stones of the riverbed. They were such beautiful shapes and colours.

There were fish as well: small pink and brown trout with curious eyes, large fish silver and lean, and long slippery eels with tiny eyes and quickly darting tongues. There were ancient, slow moving turtles who never seemed to notice much of what was going on around them. And there were tiny creatures too — animals so small they could barely be seen. All lived in the deep, swiftly moving river, and were part of it, and the river was a part of them.

There was also in this river another creature, who had lived there for a long time — so long she could no longer remember coming there, or even how she got there. This creature was different than all the rest. She was different in many ways. She was not a fish or a plant — indeed, she was much bigger than the fish and plants in the river. She knew she wasn't a fish, because although she could breathe the water, she could also breathe the air. And when she wanted she could leave the river and walk in the woods under the cold moonlight. But what made her especially different was that she was alone. She was the only one of her kind. She was the Water Witch.

For many days the Water Witch had been swimming up the river. Her swimming was effortless. She was more graceful than any fish and she was proud of her grace and strength. But she swam so quickly that she ignored all the beauty that surrounded her. Even when she saw her reflection in the water she didn't know that it, too, was beautiful. She didn't notice the plants and the coloured fish and stones, or where the river was shallow, how the sunlight warmed the running water and made the colours even more brilliant and clear.

She didn't hear the whispering whirlpools or the musical gurgle of the eddies. The Water Witch ignored all of this. She considered herself the wisest and most interesting inhabitant of the river, and that was enough for her. She shot through the water like an arrow, her beautiful black hair pulled out straight behind, her green eyes always fixed straight ahead.

One morning after the Water Witch had been swimming for a long time, she raised her head up out of the water and looked around. A few yards from shore there was a large rock. She swam over and pulled herself up on it, took out her pearl comb, and began to comb out her thick black hair. She turned her head lazily to the sun and thought how nice it was to be the Queen of the river.

In the distance there was the deep thundering of a waterfall. But then she heard another sound — voices. They were high and sweet and rang out clearly over the roar of the waterfall. Quickly, she turned in the direction of the voices, and what she saw made her stare with wonder.

FOR MANY DAYS THE WATER WITCH HAD BEEN SWIMMING UP THE RIVER.

Near the waterfall there were figures moving: two — no, three. What were they? Silently, she slid into the water and swam slowly towards the waterfall, taking care to keep out of sight. Were they seals? No, seals didn't sound like that, and besides, they only lived in the ocean. She sank beneath the water and swam closer and closer.

When she surfaced, she hid behind a large rock and peeped around it at creatures she had never seen before. She was surprised to see that they looked much as she did — except that two of them were also like fish. They darted through the water, laughing and splashing. It was very curious. But the other creature interested her even more. This one didn't have a tail, and was very much like the Water Witch herself, except she was smaller and had brilliant yellow hair.

As the Water Witch looked at her, she sensed that this was a very powerful creature, and began to feel uneasy. Who were they, and what were they doing? She looked one last time at the strangers and slid silently beneath the water. She had to find out who they were.

All that night the Water Witch circled slowly in the deepest part of the river and brooded. The nerve of those creatures to come into her river. Well, they wouldn't be there for long — not if she had anything to say about it. The little fishlike ones didn't concern her greatly, but the other one, the one with the yellow hair, she was different. Could they be just visiting? No, they looked very much at home. Perhaps they meant to drive her out and live in the river by themselves? Well, if that was the case she wouldn't give up without a fight. She'd show them who was the owner of the river. But first she needed to know more about the one with the yellow hair. The Water Witch thought and thought, and in a little while she knew what to do.

Chapter 3

For the first time in days Greta was cheerful. That morning she had finally begun to look at the bright side of things and not be sad that she would be leaving. She decided to pick a fragrant bouquet of water lilies as a going-away present for Amanda Greenleaf, and then she and Glinka would swim down this wonderful river until they reached the wide salt ocean. There they would regain their strength and see all the other merpeople, and the huge whales and fish that lived there. It would be nice. In a very little while, they would return to the river and waterfall and the best friend they ever had.

Greta swam lazily on her back and dreamed about the whales. Suddenly she heard a low whistling sound. It seemed to be coming from behind a large rock. She hovered in the water and listened. Then she heard laughter — high, sweet laughter. It reminded her of the little merchildren in the ocean. 'But it couldn't be,' she said to herself. 'What would a merchild be doing here?' Greta began to move slowly in the direction of the rock. The laughter continued, and then she heard muffled giggling, as if someone didn't want to be heard. She drifted closer until she was only inches from the rock.

"Who's there?" she called softly. The murmuring and laughter stopped for a second, but then it continued as before.

"Hello," Greta called shyly. "Amanda Greenleaf, is that you? Are you playing a joke on me?" She placed her hands on the rock and peered over the edge. When she screamed, no one heard her for the thundering of the waterfall.

Greta had expected to see a young child; instead she saw a woman — a most extraordinary woman. She had thick black hair and very red lips. Her cheekbones were high, and her eyebrows sharp and thin. But what fascinated Greta was her eyes: they were beautifully shaped and curved like fish. In the middle of each eye was a waterfall — a leaping green waterfall that tumbled and splashed. When she looked into those eyes it was impossible to turn away. Greta was transfixed. All she could see were teeming green waterfalls.

The woman began to speak in a high, light voice. "Come, my pretty little one," she said. "Look into the waterfalls in my eyes ... listen to the sound of the water crashing around you ... look deeply into the lovely liquid green ... isn't it delicious ... isn't it, my darling?"

Greta's eyes opened as wide as saucers. "Yes," she agreed faintly. "It's wonderful."

"Of course it is," said the woman. "Now my little one, you must tell me what you are."

"Why, I'm a mermaid," Greta replied.

"A mermaid?" said the woman, and for an instant something flickered in her memory. "A mermaid," she repeated slowly. "How interesting." The woman moved closer to Greta. "Wouldn't you like to come visit me? Wouldn't you love to swim in these lovely green waters? Of course you would! Now close your eyes and go to sleep. When you awaken you'll be in my home. Then you will tell me everything you know; what you're doing here, and especially you must tell me about the one with the yellow hair. You must tell me about her power and where it comes from. Can you do that for the Water Witch?"

Greta nodded her head slowly.

"Of course you can, my little mermaid. Now take my hand, for we have far to go."

The Water Witch reached out her hand. Greta took it willingly. Then they both sank beneath the dark water and began to swim quickly downstream.

Chapter 4

"Oh, Greta!" Glinka called. "Come and see the stones. They're beautiful."

Glinka swam to a flat ledge near the foot of the waterfall and deposited a heap of brightly coloured stones. "Orange, red, blue — my, they're lovely." He turned and called again, "Greta! You're so slow. Come and see." There was no answer.

'That's funny,' he thought. 'It doesn't take that long to pick water lilies.' He swam out to the middle of the pool and looked all around. Greta was nowhere to be seen. He swam slowly down the river, calling and looking behind the rocks.

Suddenly, a strange feeling crept over him and he became very frightened. "Greta, where are you!" he cried loudly. Still there was no answer. He turned and raced back to the waterfall.

"Amanda Greenleaf, come quickly!" he cried. Amanda Greenleaf rushed out. She had never heard Glinka sound so excited. When she saw his face she knew something was terribly wrong.

"Have you seen Greta?" he asked breathlessly.

"No, not for a few hours. I've been experimenting with my harp."

"Oh, Amanda Greenleaf, she's gone! I can't find her anywhere!"

"Gone? But where could she go?"

"I don't know. She went to pick water lilies and I went to find stones for the basket. I wanted to see which ones she liked best, the red ones or the blue ones, but when I went to ask her she was gone and then ..."

"Glinka, you're going too fast!" cried Amanda Greenleaf. "Slow down and start at the beginning."

Glinka took a deep breath. He looked very worried. "We wanted to make a bouquet of water lilies for you. It was a going-away present. Greta said she knew a place a little way down the river where there were some beautiful ones. She went to get them. I dove down to the bottom to collect some coloured stones to decorate the basket, but when I came up I couldn't find her anywhere. I've been calling and calling. Where could she be?"

"I don't know," Amanda Greenleaf answered. "Take me to the place where the water lilies are."

She dove into the pool and Glinka led her down the river.

"It was around here," he said. "Look, there's the patch of water lilies. But they haven't been touched. Greta! Oh, Greta, where are you?" he called.

Amanda Greenleaf circled slowly in the water and looked carefully around her. The river flowed on peacefully as it had always done, but she felt something very strange. She took her green leaf in her hand and shut her eyes tightly. Immediately, the image of Greta appeared before her, but she looked different somehow. Her eyes were dreamy and heavy with sleep. And there was someone else, too, but Amanda Greenleaf couldn't make out who it was. The image faded and she felt Glinka shaking her arm.

"What happened?" he asked. "You're so pale. Did you see Greta? Do you know where she is?"

"Yes, I saw her, but I don't know where she is. Only that she has gone down the river."

Glinka stared at Amanda Greenleaf in disbelief. "But she wouldn't leave without me. Why would she go by herself?"

Amanda Greenleaf looked seriously at Glinka. "Glinka, Greta isn't alone," she said quietly. "I think someone has taken her."

"But who would do such a thing? Why would anyone want to take Greta?"

"I don't know."

"We must go and find her right away — there isn't a moment to lose!" said Glinka, turning to swim away.

"Wait a minute," said Amanda Greenleaf, taking him by the arm.

"But we can't wait," he said earnestly. "Amanda Greenleaf — remember — we're running out of time. The moon is nearly full."

"I know," Amanda Greenleaf said firmly. "But there's no point in blindly rushing off. We need to know more."

"But what else can we do?"

"One thing we mustn't do is panic," she said. "We must stop and make a plan." She swam in a slow circle, concentrating very hard.

Glinka watched her in silence, until he couldn't contain himself any longer. "Amanda Greenleaf, if you're going to make a plan, could you please make it now!"

Amanda Greenleaf looked at him reassuringly. "There is someone who may know what's happened," she said. "Come, we must go back to the waterfall."

Chapter 5

There's nothing more magical than the song of the waterfall. It's not just one sound, but a great many sounds all being played together. At the bottom the water roars and thunders in a thick heavy pounding as it drums against the rocks. But there are high sounds, too — a continuous wet hissing like water being thrown on a fire. Scattered throughout, quite on their own almost, little rivulets pop and splash. There's even a sound in the spray, a heavy dripping sound in the white mist. All of these sounds and many more make up the song of the waterfall.

Amanda Greenleaf swam up to the foot of the waterfall and pulled herself up on the rocks until she stood exactly in the middle. The water poured down over her so that it seemed as if she became part of the waterfall. At first Glinka could see her very plainly. Her yellow hair and green dress stood out against the falling water. Then she seemed to disappear. Her hair turned to twisting rivulets, the green of her dress dissolved into the dark green of the water. When she spread her hands, her fingers turned frothy white and themselves became little waterfalls.

Amanda Greenleaf closed her eyes and felt the water flow through her. She concentrated all of her attention on the rushing voice of the waterfall. She could no longer feel her arms or legs. When she had been part of the waterfall for a little while, a deep clear voice began to rise up out of the depths.

"Hello, Amanda Greenleaf, Guardian of the Waterfall. Do you have something to ask me?"

Amanda Greenleaf knew it was the voice of the Water Spirit. "Yes," she replied, "it's very important. Our friend, Greta the mermaid, has been taken away. I want to know who did this and why, and if you know where she is."

For a moment there was no answer. Then the voice said: "She has been taken by a witch who lives in the river, the Water Witch."

"What's a witch?" Amanda Greenleaf asked.

"A witch is someone who has power but who uses it badly."

"Why would anyone do that?"

"That's a difficult question," the Water Spirit replied. "With this witch, I don't know. She is very old, and it could be that she has been alone too long, and has forgotten how to behave. There may be many reasons."

"*You* don't know?" Amanda Greenleaf asked in amazement. "I thought you knew everything."

"In this world there are many mysteries," said the Water Spirit. "You are one yourself. Some can be understood, some can't — at least not fully."

"Do you know the Water Witch?" asked Amanda Greenleaf.

"Once I knew her well, but we haven't talked in a long time. Amanda Greenleaf, it's up to you to unravel this mystery."

"Why me?"

"Because in many ways you are much alike."

"Do you mean I'm a witch, too?"

"No. But even you could become one."

WHEN SHE HAD BEEN PART OF THE WATERFALL
FOR A LITTLE WHILE, A DEEP CLEAR VOICE BEGAN TO RISE
OUT OF THE DEPTHS.

Amanda Greenleaf didn't know what to say. She felt very worried and confused.

"Is the Water Witch more powerful than I am?" she asked quietly.

"That remains to be seen. Her power is deep and old and she knows many spells."

"Can you help me?"

"I already have. You have your chain and leaf."

"What if that's not enough?" Amanda Greenleaf said nervously.

"You also have your love for the mermaid," said the Water Spirit.

"Yes," she said. "I have that. But there is so little time. Soon the moon will be full and then ..."

"Her fate is in your hands."

"Does this ... witch have a name?" asked Amanda Greenleaf.

"At one time she did, though I fear she has forgotten it. But it used to be Miranda."

Amanda Greenleaf remained silent. There was so much to understand. Gradually, she felt herself return to normal. Glinka was waiting expectantly for her. She dove down into the pool and swam up next to him.

"Did you find out anything?" he asked eagerly.

Amanda Greenleaf nodded. "Yes. Greta has been taken by a water witch. We don't know why."

Glinka's face clouded. "A witch?" he said. "Whatever in the world is a witch?"

"I'm not exactly sure," Amanda Greenleaf said. "But this one is called Miranda."

Chapter 6

Amanda Greenleaf and Glinka swam through the night, never pausing, constantly scanning the water and the riverbank for any sign of their friend. But there was nothing — just deep dark water, and black boulders and trees. 'Of all the times to be stolen by a witch,' Glinka thought miserably. 'Not that therc's a good time, I suppose. Oh, we never should have stayed so long.' He looked up at the moon. Soon it would be perfectly full.

The next morning when the sky turned pink over the hilltops and the first birds began to chatter in the woods, Glinka turned to Amanda Greenleaf. "Do you think we can take a little rest?" he asked. "We've been swimming all night."

She was surprised to hear him say that, for she knew how badly he wanted to find Greta. But he looked pale and tired. 'This is strange,' she thought. 'Merpeople can usually swim for days and days and not get tired.' But then she realized that the water was affecting Glinka already.

They stopped in the river. Amanda Greenleaf climbed up on a flat rock and helped Glinka up beside her. He was breathing very hard. He curled his tail beneath him and smiled weakly. "I'll be all right," he said. "Just give me a minute."

Amanda Greenleaf looked all around. Here the river was narrow and shallow. Brambles and green alders grew down to the water's edge. Long grasses bent in the breeze and there were fragrant water lilies everywhere. Dead tree tops poked up out of the water spreading their grey-white branches. Suddenly, something moved near the riverbank. There was a fluttering, slapping sound. Then it grew still again.

"Glinka, did you hear that?" Amanda Greenleaf whispered.

Glinka nodded. "Yes, it's over there."

"Shh!" she whispered. "You stay here. I'm going to see what it is."

"Be careful!" called Glinka softly. "Don't you get taken, too!"

Amanda Greenleaf glided silently away. As she drew near the shore, the water became too shallow to swim in, and she was forced to stand up and creep as quietly as she could.

The fluttering started again and she froze in her tracks. She held her green leaf in her hand for protection and peered ahead, but she couldn't see anything. As she took a step forward, she heard a loud sigh, and a voice said: "Oh dear, oh dear, oh dear." It was a nice voice; it sounded like a gurgling spring. It was not a voice to be afraid of, so Amanda Greenleaf crept closer. Then she saw a most curious thing. It was a trout. But he wasn't in the river. He was perched on some brambles that grew out of the shallow water. The trout twisted and flipped vigorously from side to side, but it was no use. He simply could not get back into the water. "And all for a fly," the trout sighed. "I always did have a weakness for flies. Well, I guess I jumped after one fly too many. Oh dear, oh dear, oh dear."

Amanda Greenleaf moved closer to the trout and for the first time it struck her as odd that a trout should be talking. She looked down and noticed that she was holding her green leaf in her right hand. She dropped the leaf and immediately the trout became silent. She grasped the leaf again and the trout said: "I never thought it would end like this — stranded high and dry on a branch. Oh dear."

Amanda Greenleaf crouched down next to the trout. "You poor little thing. However did you get yourself in such trouble?"

The trout was so startled that he jumped and he almost *did* fall back into the river. For a moment he looked frightened, but then he cleared his throat and gathered himself together. "I don't know who, or indeed what you are," he gurgled, "but I wonder if you would be so kind as to put me back in the water."

"Why, I would be happy to," said Amanda Greenleaf.

"Mind you wet your hands first," said the trout.

She dipped her hands in the water and carefully picked up the trout. Already he had grown very dry, and she didn't like to think what would have happened if he had been there much longer. She placed him gently back in the water.

"Ooh, that feels goooooddddd!" he sighed. Gradually his tail and fins began to twitch back and forth and he swam slowly out to the deep water. Amanda Greenleaf followed. The trout looked surprised when he saw her swimming along next to him. "My," he said, "you swim very well for a ... ah, excuse me, but what exactly are you?"

She laughed. "My name is Amanda Greenleaf. I'm many things. I'm a girl, but I'm also the Guardian of the Waterfall."

The trout didn't really understand any of this. "Hmm, I've never had much use for waterfalls. They always get in your way when you're going somewhere. But thank you very much for saving me."

"How did you get tangled up in those branches? I thought fish only liked the water?"

"Well, we do," said the trout. "But I'm very fond of two things: jumping and flies. There's nothing I like better. I had been chasing this beautiful fat blue fly all across the river, and when I finally caught up to it I had to jump as hard and high as I could. I got the fly, but unfortunately, I didn't land back in the water. I had jumped so far that I landed on those infernal branches. I'm lucky you came along."

"I'm glad I did, too," said Amanda Greenleaf.

"By the way," said the trout, "do you have any relatives around here? I saw someone else like you yesterday. At least I think she was like you, but she was moving too fast for me to really notice. I've seen her before but I always take care to stay out of her way."

Suddenly Glinka swam up to them. "Amanda Greenleaf, are you all right? You were gone such a long time."

"Yes, I'm fine," she said. "Look. I've found a new friend."

The trout looked at Glinka and jumped out of the water with fright. "Well, nice to meet you," he said nervously. "I really must be going now." And he swam away as fast as his fins would take him.

"Oh, don't go!" Amanda Greenleaf cried. "There's so much I have to ask you." But the trout had disappeared into the deep water. "Oh, I wish he hadn't gone. He told me that he had seen something strange yesterday."

"Do you think it might have been Greta and the witch?" asked Glinka.

"I don't know. It could have been. Oh, why did he leave so suddenly?"

Glinka looked embarrassed. "I think it might have been me. Sometimes fish who aren't used to merpeople think we're going to eat them. They think we're just big hungry fish."

"What bad luck," said Amanda Greenleaf. "Maybe he could have told us something."

"I have an idea," said Glinka. "I'll swim away and perhaps he'll come back if you call him."

Amanda Greenleaf waited until he was out of sight and grasped her green leaf tightly in her hand. "Oh, little trout, please come back and talk to me. We won't hurt you. Didn't I already save you from the brambles? Please little trout, I need to ask you something."

She waited patiently, but nothing happened. Then, just as she was about to give up hope, she heard a loud splash, and in the distance she could see the trout darting this way and that through the water. "Yes, little trout, I'm over here," she called. The trout swam nearer but he stopped safely out of reach. "You can come closer. Glinka isn't here."

The trout looked carefully around with his colourful round eyes. "Well, you seem all right. But that other one is frightening. What is he?"

"He's a merman."

"Does he eat fish?"

"No. Why, some of his best friends are fish."

"Hmm. I was brought up to always watch out for fish who are bigger than I am."

"But he's only half fish."

"Perhaps that half likes to eat trout."

"No," laughed Amanda Greenleaf. "You don't have to worry."

"All right, I believe you. But you can't be too careful these days. I've never seen so many strange creatures in this river before."

"Who did you see yesterday?" asked Amanda Greenleaf eagerly. "Were they like us?"

"Yes. There was one like you and one like — what did you say his name was?"

"Glinka."

"And one like Glinka, half like me and half like you. Do you know them?"

"We know the mermaid. Her name is Greta. She was taken by the other one. She's a witch," she added mysteriously.

"You're a strange lot and no mistake. Witches, mermen, mermaids, stealing each other. You certainly lead complicated lives. I just like swimming and jumping. And flies, of course."

"I must go and see Glinka," said Amanda Greenleaf. "Would you like to meet him? He won't hurt you," she added quickly.

"All right," said the trout. "If you say so."

They swam over to the rock and joined Glinka. The trout looked at him suspiciously. "Are you sure you don't eat fish?"

"No," said Glinka. "I like fish."

"That's what worries me," said the trout.

"What do you know about the Water Witch?" Amanda Greenleaf asked.

"Not much, really," he replied. "She passes through here when you least expect her. She swims straight on and disappears. Yesterday was the first time anyone was with her. She swims beautifully, much like you do."

THEY SWAM OVER TO THE ROCK AND JOINED GLINKA.

“How did Greta look?” asked Glinka.

“I couldn’t tell. They were moving too fast.”

“Do you know where she lives?” asked Amanda Greenleaf.

“No,” said the trout. “The fish further down the river might. If you’d like I’ll swim a little way with you. I could ask the other fish if they’ve seen anyone.”

“That would be wonderful,” she said.

“Well, I owe you a favour. You did save my life.” He looked nervously at Glinka. “You’re sure about ...?”

“Oh yes,” laughed Amanda Greenleaf.

“Well then, let’s go, shall we?” They turned, and with their new companion they continued down the river.

Chapter 7

Slowly Greta opened her eyes. She had no idea where she was. It was very dim and everywhere water bubbled and dripped and echoed in a strange music. The air was heavy and thick with the scent of lavender and lilac. She felt very weak and confined. Where could she be?

As her eyes grew used to the darkness, she could see a maze of tunnels and streams. She realized that she was in a small pool. It was scarcely the width of her outstretched arms. Feeling weak and dizzy, she sank beneath the water. She explored the pool and was shocked to find that there was no way out. The walls and bottom were solid rock.

'How did I get here?' she wondered. Gradually her memory cleared. She had gone to pick a bouquet of water lilies, and heard voices that sounded like the merchildren. Oh yes! Now she remembered! The woman with the green eyes who made her feel so sleepy and strange! They had swum together for a long time.

Greta knew that she had to get away. Frantically, she ran her hands up and down the sides of the walls. There had to be some way for the water to get in. She found an opening in the rock, but it was too small for her to get through. Weak and tired, she sank to the bottom of the pool, curled her tail around herself, and tried to think what to do. Sadly she noticed that the blue and turquoise scales of her tail were beginning to lose some of their brilliance. She touched her tail and several scales came away in her hand. Horrified, she shot up to the surface crying: "Amanda Greenleaf! Glinka! Where are you?"

"That, my dear, is exactly what I'd like to know," the Water Witch said calmly.

The shock of seeing the strange woman again took away Greta's voice. The Water Witch folded her arms and looked down at her, a slight smile playing across her lips.

"Who are you, and what do you want with me?" asked Greta when her voice finally came back to her.

"My, you're such an inquisitive creature," said the Water Witch. "An admirable trait for a fish — but then you're only half fish, aren't you?"

"You must let me go," Greta pleaded. "I have to get back to the ocean. I have to find my friends."

"Yes, your friends. What did you say their names were? Glinka and ... Amanda something, I believe it was. Is Amanda the one with the yellow hair?"

Greta refused to answer.

"My dear, you must be more co-operative. It will save us time. I need to know about your friend Amanda."

"I won't tell you anything," Greta said firmly.

"Oh, but you will, my dear. You will tell me how she came to be in this river, and where she gets her power, and most importantly, you will tell me what she intends to do." The Water Witch knelt down at the edge of the pool and gazed intently at Greta. Greta struggled to turn away but it was no use; she was too weak. "Now, my little mermaid, tell me about Amanda," the Water Witch continued, and teeming green waterfalls began to leap in her eyes.

Against her will, Greta began to speak, and as she did so, something magical happened. For the image of everything she said appeared in the water before her as she was describing it.

"Amanda Greenleaf did not always live in the river," Greta said. "Once she was just a little girl named Amanda who lived near the river far upstream from here. She loved the river and its magical sound."

In the water there appeared the image of a little girl walking down to a riverbank.

"One day when she had come to get water for breakfast, she stayed awhile and closed her eyes and listened to the river's soothing song. It was very pleasant by the river and she began to feel drowsy. Suddenly, she fell into the water. The river was so swift and Amanda was such a little girl that it carried her down and down. Down she went through the boiling rapids; she was tossed and turned."

The Water Witch watched, totally absorbed by the image of the struggling little girl.

"The river swept her on and on and no one heard her cries for help. Then she heard the roar of a waterfall. She struggled with every ounce of strength that was left in her, for she knew that if she was swept over the falls she would surely be killed. But it was no use. She was carried down and the water pounded over her."

The Water Witch stared, spellbound.

"That's when Glinka and I saw her," Greta continued dreamily. "We didn't know what to do or even what she was, but she looked so helpless floating in the water that we swam up to her and pushed her to shore. And that was all we could do, for merpeople cannot leave the water ..."

"Yes, yes, go on," said the Water Witch impatiently.

"We hid behind a rock and watched," said Greta. "As Amanda lay there, a voice called to her. It seemed to be coming from the waterfall. She opened her eyes and turned over and the voice told her to get up.

"We could see she was very surprised, but she walked a little way out into the river. The voice told her to come out further and not to be afraid. So she swam out and sat on a rock at the bottom of the falls. Then the voice told her to look down into the water," Greta continued. "Amanda looked down and she could just barely see something green and silver glinting far below. 'You must dive to the bottom and get the chain and leaf that lies there,' said the voice, 'for you have been chosen to be Guardian and Watcher of this river and waterfall.'

"Amanda looked unsure of herself — the water was so deep — but then she quickly dove in and headed towards the chain. Glinka and I followed her. It was a long way down to where the chain lay, but just when she could hold her breath no longer, she reached it and grasped it in her hand. And she returned safely to the surface."

"Well, that's not so difficult," said the Water Witch. "I can stay under for days."

"The voice instructed her to put on the chain," Greta went on. "When Amanda did so, she changed. Her hair turned to brilliant yellow gold, and the old brown dress she had been wearing turned to a beautiful green. A magical strength rose up in her and filled her from the tips of her toes to the strands of her golden hair. She found that she could swim beneath the water like a fish; she felt as if she were truly a part of the river. She had never been more happy in her whole life.

"Then the voice told her that she was no longer Amanda: she was Amanda Greenleaf, Guardian of the Waterfall and Watcher of the river.

“Finally, the voice told her to walk through the waterfall,” Greta went on. “Behind it she found a deep cosy cave that smelled of lilac and heather, and Amanda Greenleaf made her home there. Now she was the Guardian of the Waterfall and a friend of the Water Spirit. She also became our special friend. We liked her so much that we stayed with her for a long time. And she is ... the best ... friend ... we’ve ever had ....”

Telling the story had weakened Greta so much that she sank beneath the water. The images in the pool faded and disappeared.

The Water Witch walked slowly around the cavern. ‘How absolutely extraordinary,’ she thought. ‘A Guardian.’

It was all very strange. Still, she had found out one thing she wanted to know. It was the chain and leaf that gave the girl her special powers. If the Water Witch had that, then she had nothing to fear from Amanda Greenleaf.

Chapter 8

Glinka was steadily getting weaker. Amanda Greenleaf didn't say anything, but she knew it was becoming more and more difficult for him to keep up with them. The trout was magnificent: he streaked through the water and leaped high into the air. Even Glinka was amazed at his great jumping skill.

Whenever they met other fish, the trout would swim off and ask if they knew where the Water Witch lived. Poor Glinka had to hide every time because when the fish saw him they swam away in fright. Glinka thought that was very funny. 'I'm so weak, I wouldn't be able to catch them even if I wanted to,' he thought sadly.

But none of the other fish knew where the Water Witch came from, although they had all seen her. At last, the trout returned from one of his excursions and was very excited.

"I've just been talking to someone who knows where the Water Witch lives! He wants us to come and see him!"

"Oh, that's wonderful," cried Amanda Greenleaf.

"Should I come, too?" asked Glinka. "Won't he be scared of me?"

"He won't be scared of you," laughed the trout. "I don't think he's scared of anyone."

They followed the trout deep down to the bottom of the river. The water was murky and in the distance they could just see the outline of a rocky cave. They waited outside the cave and looked around curiously. There was a deep rumble, and something began to inch its way out from between the rocks. It was a huge turtle. He looked very old and his shell was covered with thick brown moss. His neck was wrinkled and rough. He looked at each of them in turn with great hooded eyes that blinked slowly and rhythmically. His gaze fell upon Glinka.

"So it's true," he chuckled deeply. "I haven't seen one of your kind in many long years. A merman, aren't you?"

"Why ... why, yes," stammered Glinka. "How did you know?"

"Oh, there isn't much I don't know," said the turtle in his deep voice. "When you're as old as I am, it's hard not to know things."

"How old are you?" asked Glinka curiously.

"Glinka! That's not polite," said Amanda Greenleaf.

"Oh, it's all right," laughed the turtle. "Glinka is your name, is it? Well Glinka, let's say that I'm as old as this river. I was here before there was anyone else, and I expect I'll be here long after everyone is gone." He turned to Amanda Greenleaf. "And you must be Amanda Greenleaf. Yes, I know your name, and everything about you."

"But how could you?" she asked. "I've never been here before."

"We have a mutual friend, my dear, someone who is even older than I am. Of course, I've never seen him, but we talk just the same."

"You mean the Water Spirit, don't you," she cried happily.

"Yes, the Water Spirit. He told me you might be passing this way."

"Then you know about Greta and the Water Witch. Do you know where they are?"

"Yes, I know where they are. The Water Spirit has asked me to take you there." He looked at Glinka kindly. "I fear that time may be running out for you and your friend." He shook his head and sighed heavily.

"Why did the Water Witch take Greta?" asked Amanda Greenleaf. "What could she possibly want with her?"

"I'm not sure," said the turtle thoughtfully. "But she didn't always do such foolish things. Once she was much like you. I think she became lonely, and it made her blind to the beauty around her. And, Amanda Greenleaf," the turtle added seriously, "I don't think the Water Witch is interested in Greta. I think she's interested in you."

"Me?"

"Yes. She may be using Greta to trap you. You are very much on her mind. I think she may be afraid of you."

"Afraid of *me*?" said Amanda Greenleaf. "But that's silly!"

"Perhaps," said the turtle. "Hopefully, you can help her and save the mermaid at the same time."

"But how?" she asked.

"That's for you to decide. Come now. It's my task to show you where you can find her."

The turtle swam off in his slow, deliberate fashion. Amanda Greenleaf, Glinka, and the trout followed closely. The turtle moved gracefully and serenely for such a heavy creature.

THE TURTLE SWAM OFF
IN HIS SLOW, DELIBERATE FASHION.

As they swam, Glinka turned to Amanda Greenleaf. "It's all very well that we seem to have found Greta," he said. "But how in the world are we going to get her away from the Water Witch?"

Amanda Greenleaf looked troubled. "I'm not sure," she said. "I've never had to do anything like this before. We'll just have to have faith in ourselves." She grasped her chain and leaf. "And in this," she added.

Glinka looked at her and nodded. "Well, I hope we do it quickly," he said quietly. He stopped and pointed at the tip of his tail. Already it was beginning to turn white.

The turtle led them on through the deep murky water. Amanda Greenleaf was worried and frightened. She didn't know what to expect from a Water Witch. And poor Greta! She must be so scared. She looked at Glinka. He was trying hard, but he could scarcely keep his head up to see where he was swimming. Even the trout looked troubled as he darted quickly through the water.

Finally, they stopped before a crumbling rock wall that had a dark tunnel leading through it. "This is the way," said the turtle. "The tunnel leads to a maze of underwater caves and hot springs. That's the home of the Water Witch, and that's where she has brought your friend."

Amanda Greenleaf and Glinka looked cautiously into the tunnel. "Can you come with us?" she asked the turtle.

He shook his head. "No. My task is finished. Now it's up to you and your companions."

"I'll come," said the trout. "I've always been interested in that Water Witch." But his voice was shaking as he spoke.

Amanda Greenleaf looked into the tunnel. "Well, we'd better go, hadn't we? Greta is waiting for us. Thank you so much," she said to the turtle. The turtle nodded his head. Amanda Greenleaf smiled bravely and entered the dark tunnel.

Chapter 9

The tunnel continued for a long way. It was very dark. Amanda Greenleaf kept her hands out in front of her so she wouldn't bump into anything. No one spoke. The only sound was Glinka's heavy breathing.

After awhile the water began to turn dark green, then a lighter green, and Amanda Greenleaf knew they were coming to the end of the tunnel. At length they emerged into a deep pool. She looked up towards the surface and saw that they were in a large cavern. She turned to Glinka and the trout. "You stay here. I'm going to surface and look around."

"I want to come," said the trout.

"No. You must stay with Glinka. I'll come back and tell you what I find."

She began to swim slowly upwards. When she reached the surface she raised her head up into the air and looked carefully around. Everywhere there were streams and pools of different sizes, and many tunnels leading off in all directions. The cavern echoed with the sound of falling water. Hot springs bubbled through cracks in the rock walls, and fountains pushed up through the ground. It was sticky and warm and the air hung still and misty. The cavern was very bare, just rock and water. Amanda Greenleaf climbed up onto the bank. The splashing of water was the only sound.

Slowly she crept forward, her heart pounding in her chest. She moved carefully, her eyes darting from side to side. Then she saw Greta. She was in a small pool and appeared to be sleeping. She was only half in the water, her head resting on the edge. Amanda Greenleaf stifled a cry of delight and ran up to her.

"Greta, are you all right?" she whispered.

Greta's eyes flickered open. "Oh, Amanda Greenleaf, I knew you'd come," she said weakly.

Amanda Greenleaf bent down on her knees and stroked Greta's hair. "It's all right," she said soothingly. "We'll soon get you out." She looked deeply into Greta's eyes. But there was something strange about them.

Suddenly, tiny green waterfalls began to leap up in each of Greta's eyes. Her hand flashed up and with blinding speed she took hold of Amanda Greenleaf's chain and pulled it over her head. "Greta!" Amanda Greenleaf screamed, but then she realized that it was not Greta at all. Greta dissolved before her and in her place was a woman — a woman with long black hair and magical green eyes. She held Amanda Greenleaf's chain and leaf in her hand.

"Hello, Amanda Greenleaf," the Water Witch said. "I've been expecting you." Amanda Greenleaf was hypnotized by the Water Witch's eyes. She couldn't turn away. She began to feel dizzy. Everything went black and she fell down into the water.

Amanda Greenleaf sank slowly towards the bottom of the pool. She knew she should fight her way back to the surface, but she felt so very tired. It was easier to just drift to the bottom. She felt very sleepy, and was just about to close her eyes when something stirred below her. She looked down. There was someone lying at the bottom of the pool. She had beautiful long hair with golden combs in it, and a graceful blue and turquoise tail. But there were small white patches on the tail.

Suddenly, Amanda Greenleaf snapped out of her daze. It was Greta! There was no doubt that this was the real Greta. Quickly she gathered her thoughts together. The Water Witch had taken her chain and leaf. She had to get back to the surface before she ran out of air. But what about Greta? There was only one way — she had to save herself first. She kicked her legs strongly and began to swim up to the surface.

When Amanda Greenleaf broke through the water gasping for air, the Water Witch was sitting at the edge of the pool watching her. In her hand she held the chain and leaf.

"So you're Amanda Greenleaf," the Water Witch said. "How do you like my home?"

Amanda Greenleaf looked up at her intently. The Water Witch looked very severe with her strange eyes and haughty expression. But still she didn't look like an evil person.

"Why are you doing this?" asked Amanda Greenleaf. "We've never done anything to you."

"Never done anything to me?" the Water Witch echoed bitterly. "Perhaps not. But who's to say that you wouldn't — that you weren't planning to. Besides, this is my river. You and your friends are not welcome here."

"But no one owns the river," Amanda Greenleaf replied. "It exists for everyone, the fish and plants ..."

"And it can only have one ruler," the Water Witch interrupted. "I've always ruled here and no one else."

"Didn't you ever get lonely?" asked Amanda Greenleaf.

"Lonely? What do you mean?"

"SO YOU'RE AMANDA GREENLEAF," THE WATER WITCH SAID.
"HOW DO YOU LIKE MY HOME?"

"Didn't you miss talking to other creatures and sharing things with them? That's what this river and all the beautiful things in the world are for, to share."

The Water Witch laughed. "I've no idea what you're talking about. And besides, how do you explain this?" she asked, holding up the chain and leaf. "This gives you great power. What do you intend to do with so much power?"

"I'm a Guardian," answered Amanda Greenleaf. "The chain and leaf have been entrusted to me for the protection of this river and its inhabitants."

"Do you really expect me to believe that you weren't planning to drive me away from here?" said the Water Witch sarcastically.

"Why would I want to do that?" asked Amanda Greenleaf. "I would love to have another friend to share things with, and learn things from. A friend like Greta and Glinka. Haven't you *ever* had any friends?"

The Water Witch didn't answer but she stood up and for a moment it seemed as if she were remembering something from deep in her past.

"Friends," she murmured. "Yes, maybe I did have friends once. But it was long ago." The memory flickered and disappeared, and the suspicious expression returned to her face.

"I'm keeping you and your friend here until I know what you're planning."

"But you can't," cried Amanda Greenleaf. "Greta and Glinka must get back to the ocean or ... or they'll both die."

For a moment the Water Witch looked confused. Then her face hardened and she laughed grimly. "I don't think you're going anywhere without this," she said, holding up the chain and leaf.

Suddenly, there was a sharp splash and something leaped straight up out of the water. It was the trout. As he leaped, he snatched the chain and leaf right out of the hand of the Water Witch. When he fell back towards the water he released it and it fell over Amanda Greenleaf's head. Immediately, she closed her hand around the leaf and felt her strength surging back into her. The Water Witch stepped back in horror. Then she turned and ran quickly down one of the dark tunnels.

Chapter 10

"What a jump!" cried the trout with pride. "It was brilliant. That's the highest I've ever gone!"

"How did you find me?" asked Amanda Greenleaf breathlessly. "How did you get into the pool?"

"When you didn't come back I went looking for you. I heard the Water Witch talking to you and saw that she had taken your chain and leaf. I didn't know how to get into the pool, but I searched and searched until I found a small hole that was just big enough for me to swim through."

"How's Glinka?" asked Amanda Greenleaf.

"He's much worse. He's lying on the bottom and his tail is almost completely white. Did you find Greta?"

"Yes. She's down there. She's so weak, I don't think she can swim anymore."

"We have to get them to the ocean," said the trout. "What are we going to do?"

"I don't know," Amanda Greenleaf replied. "I'm only strong enough to carry one."

"There must be a way," said the trout.

Amanda Greenleaf remembered the Water Spirit. She sank beneath the surface, closed her eyes, and concentrated. "Oh, please tell me what to do," she whispered. "There's so little time."

"Amanda Greenleaf, you have done much for the love of your friends," spoke the Water Spirit. "And now, if you wish to save them, you must ask someone to help you."

"But who? There's no one here."

"There is someone you can ask," said the Water Spirit.

"Do you mean ...?"

"Yes. You must persuade the Water Witch to help you. It's the only hope Greta and Glinka have."

"But she's the cause of all this trouble."

"Perhaps only a part of her caused this. I think there may be a part of her that's willing to help you. It's the only chance you have."

Amanda Greenleaf flew like the wind down the tunnel the Water Witch had taken. Now their enemy was their only hope. She had to find her. The tunnel led deeply through the grey rock. Suddenly, she came upon a maze of tunnels winding in all directions. Which was the right one? She took hold of her green leaf. At once one of the tunnels began to glimmer softly. Amanda Greenleaf rushed along it.

After awhile the tunnel opened out into a huge cavern. The walls were green with wet moss, and colourful flowers brightened the shadows. Long vines dangled down over the water, and small waterfalls streamed and bubbled through the rocks. In the centre, a giant white shell formed a majestic throne. The throne was empty, yet Amanda Greenleaf knew that the Water Witch was hiding nearby.

"Hello!" she cried, her voice echoing. "Please don't be afraid. I need to talk to you. I need your help."

There was no answer, just the sound of bubbling water. "Oh please!" she cried again. "Greta and Glinka are dying. We have to get them back to the ocean." But again there was no answer. "Oh, why won't you trust me?" she said sadly.

Then she knew what she had to do. "I know you can see me," she called. "Watch!" She reached up and took off her chain and leaf and carefully placed them on a stone beside her. "You see, I don't want to fight with you," she said gently. "Can't you see that we can help each other? Can't you understand that?"

There was a splashing sound and the Water Witch walked from beneath one of the small waterfalls. "We have a lot in common," smiled Amanda Greenleaf. "I like waterfalls, too." The Water Witch stared at her silently. Then she glanced over at the chain and leaf. She took a step towards Amanda Greenleaf. Then another, and another. She looked very troubled and doubtful. Finally, she was standing right before her.

"You're a strange creature, Amanda Greenleaf," she said. Quick as lightning she reached out, swept up the chain and leaf, and hid it safely within the folds of her gown. She turned and arranged herself regally upon her throne.

Amanda Greenleaf didn't move. She looked straight at the Water Witch. "I know you'll do the right thing, Miranda," she said softly.

The Water Witch looked surprised and her mouth fell open in amazement. It had been such a long time since she had heard her name.

"You weren't always a witch, were you, Miranda?" Amanda Greenleaf asked. "That's your name, isn't it? Can you remember when you were just Miranda?"

The Water Witch looked confused. It seemed as if something deep inside of her was struggling to get out. She gazed at Amanda Greenleaf steadily. Then her eyes grew clear and untroubled.

"Yes," she said slowly. "I remember."

She stood and placed the chain and leaf over Amanda Greenleaf's head. Amanda Greenleaf smiled and took Miranda's hand. "Come," she said. "We must be swifter than we've ever been before."

Outside the sun was setting, and the cold white moon began to gleam brightly against the azure sky. In a few hours it would finish its cycle and become completely full. Amanda Greenleaf didn't look up at it. She knew that their time had almost run out. But still she refused to give up hope. She thought only of swimming and speed. In her arms she held Glinka. He was growing lighter all the time and his beautiful tail had turned almost as white as the moon that shone above them. Next to them swam Miranda with Greta. The trout darted ahead, anxious to bring the news that they had finally reached the ocean.

As they swam, Miranda looked down at Greta. She was sorry that she had acted so foolishly. Well, there was still time to make it up. She kicked her legs strongly and sped on down the river.

On and on they went, and then the trout came leaping towards them. "I think we're nearly there!" he cried. "I caught a glimpse of something huge and blue between the hills."

"That's it," said Miranda. "It's just around that bend. We'll soon be there." She looked down at Greta with concern. "Do you think we'll make it?"

Amanda Greenleaf was so worried that she couldn't answer. They rounded the final bend in the river and stopped abruptly. Amanda Greenleaf's heart sank like a stone. Everyone stared ahead in shocked silence. For although the ocean was there, it seemed far away; the river had narrowed to a mere trickle. A vast expanse of dry land separated them from the ocean.

"What can it mean?" cried Amanda Greenleaf. "Has someone stolen part of the ocean?"

Miranda glanced quickly at the moon. "No," she answered slowly. "It's the tide — the tide is out. The water won't come back in for hours."

"What will we do?" asked Amanda Greenleaf, her voice shaking. "I could never carry Glinka that far."

For the first time she was completely without hope. Greta and Glinka were on the verge of dissolving into foam. She couldn't bear to think of it. And they had come so close! But now she didn't know what to do.

Miranda swam quickly towards her. "Here," she said frantically. "Take Greta."

"Where are you going?"

Miranda didn't answer. She swam towards the shore and climbed nimbly up the riverbank.

"I have power, too," she called to Amanda Greenleaf. "Spells from long ago. I had almost forgotten, but now ... now I must remember."

Miranda turned her head majestically to the moon. Even from the river Amanda Greenleaf could see her liquid green eyes. Then the green disappeared, and in each eye grew the image of a round white moon. Miranda raised her arms and the moon in the sky began to move. It dipped slightly towards the ground. As it did, Amanda Greenleaf heard a roar, a deep rumbling as if the earth had cracked open. She looked out towards the ocean and saw huge white waves rolling towards the shore and covering up the dry land. Miranda stood looking up at the sky.

As the ocean water poured in to meet the river, Amanda Greenleaf cried out to her and Miranda dove back into the river and gathered up Greta in her arms. Then they turned and swam out to meet the crashing salt waves. The ocean washed over them all. Gradually, Greta

*MIRANDA TURNED HER HEAD
MAJESTICALLY TO THE MOON.*

and Glinka's tails began to turn blue and turquoise, and their silvery scales began to sparkle. Soon they were shaking their heads and rubbing their eyes as if awakening from a long sleep. Finally, they opened their eyes widely and smiled up at Amanda Greenleaf.

"Are we home yet?" Greta asked softly.

Amanda Greenleaf looked at Miranda and the trout, and smiled down at Greta and Glinka.

"Yes," she said. "You're home."